Joy Is the Payment

M. Anetta Keys

AuthorHouse™ LLC
1663 Liberty Drive
Bloomington, IN 47403
www.authorhouse.com
Phone: 1-800-839-8640

Published by AuthorHouse 09/19/2014

ISBN: 978-1-4969-3861-9 (sc)
ISBN: 978-1-4969-3862-6 (e)

Library of Congress Control Number: 2014916289

Any people depicted in stock imagery provided by Thinkstock are models,
and such images are being used for illustrative purposes only.
Certain stock imagery © Thinkstock.

This book is printed on acid-free paper.

Because of the dynamic nature of the Internet, any web addresses or links contained in this book may have changed
since publication and may no longer be valid. The views expressed in this work are solely those of the author and do not
necessarily reflect the views of the publisher, and the publisher hereby disclaims any responsibility for them.

authorHOUSE®

Acknowledgements

I thank God for all things. My gratitude and love to my family and friends for prayers and support. My parents for teaching me God gives abundantly to his children. My son and daughter this book is dedicated to you, you're the spot light and joy of each story. My husband, you're unconditional love and gentle push to step out on faith has been just one of many gifts I receive from you. Blessings and love to you all.

Trashman Smile

I'm on summer break from school, and I see Mr. Thomas every Wednesday morning between eight and eight fifteen. He always looks so glad to be picking up the neighborhood trash.

I think to myself, *Why would anybody be smiling about picking up trash? I, for one, don't even like to take out the trash. If my mom didn't remind me, I'm sure I'd forget most of the time. So why is Mr. Thomas so happy to pick it up?*

My family and I have been in this neighborhood for about a year. We saw Mr. Thomas for the first time last summer. He would come by in his truck every Wednesday morning, waving and saying, "Good morning!" Mom and Mr. Thomas introduced themselves. Mom told Mr. Thomas that she had a son and a daughter. I guess she also gave him our names. Whenever we were outside after that, he'd say hello and call us by our names.

As I look out my bedroom window, I think to myself, *Next Wednesday, I'll make sure I'm outside when he comes by. I'm going to ask, "Mr. Thomas, what are you so happy about?" Well, maybe not. It depends on how I feel that morning. I may not care next Wednesday why he's so happy.*

A week later, I don't take out the trash because I need a good excuse to run outside when Mr. Thomas's truck comes by. I guess my mom forgot, too, because she didn't remind me last night. I'm glad about that. If she had, I would have to think up some other reason to be outside. I guess I feel like finding out why Mr. Thomas is always smiling.

The truck comes down the street, and Mr. Thomas picks up trashcan after trashcan and empties them in his not-so-big truck. There are two more houses before my house, so this is a good time to start walking toward the street with our trashcan.

"Good morning, young man," Mr. Thomas says with that smile on his face.

"Good morning," I say back.

"So do you have great plans for the summer, young man?"

"Yes, sir."

I hope he isn't going to ask me what my plans are. I really just have some great ideas.

Before I could ask my longing question, Mr. Thomas begins to tell me how much he likes to pick up the trash in my neighborhood. "This is a wonderful neighborhood you're blessed to live in, and it's always good to see a young man like yourself helping his family. The parents on this street always say how their kids do what they are asked to do. It isn't always with a smile, but the job gets done."

This is a perfect time to ask why a smile is always on his face when he picks up the trash.

But again, before I could get out the question, Mr. Thomas says, "I'm so glad to have this job. I've been told I have a smile on my face that people just don't understand."

Wow, he is making this really easy for me, I think.

"Let me tell you why. When I was a young man working for a big company in the city for about eight years, I got a letter from the CEO saying they were downsizing the company. They were sorry, but they had to let me go. I was pretty upset about the news and just didn't know how I would make enough money to take care of a wife, a little boy, and another child on the way. I had given my life to God only a year before I had to leave the company, and I was not sure why He was allowing this to happen to me. So I got on my knees that night after losing my job and asked God to please help me find a job soon. The next day, one of my father's friends needed another hand to pick up trash, so he gave me the job."

So why do you keep the smile on your face? I think.

And before the thought leaves my mind, Mr. Thomas says, "See, son, when God gives you something, it is the best, regardless of what you or others think about it. He knows just what you need when you need it. I'm also a preacher at Keys to Life Church across town. I always let the people know that your life only begins when you give God the keys to it and you let Him drive you in the direction He wants you to go."

Before I knew it, I said "Mr. Thomas, are you saying that your smile on your face is because God gave you a job as a trashman?

"You got it, Maurice," Mr. Thomas says with a great deal of excitement. "I don't make as much money as I did at the company, yet my family has all we need, and I'm enjoying doing this job more than any other job I got on my own."

"Mr. Thomas, I now understand why you smile the way you do. See, I've been told I smile a lot when I play drums, and I know my talent to play comes from God. The joy I feel to share my talent with others keeps a smile on my face too."

"Son, you're now on your way to a great future. Your future is great. You know at your young age that God is the beginning and end of all that is good and perfect in our lives."

"Thank you, sir. I now know that I'll think of your story when I see people with a smile or expression on their faces that I may not understand, and I'll think they must have a great story too."

"You have a good day, Maurice."

"I will. You too, Mr. Thomas, and keep smiling."

That was unexpected. I really didn't know what I would hear from Mr. Thomas. It is something I would remember. And the next time I see someone doing or saying something that is odd but good at the same time, I'll think, *There goes another Mr. Thomas.*

Joy Is the Payment

Mrs. Lemon has been a volunteer for my school for at least five years, maybe longer. I just know that, when I came to this school, Mrs. Lemon was already here.

Mrs. Lemon comes to my class on Tuesday and Thursday every week, and she volunteers in my friend Samantha's class the other days. Mrs. Lemon helps my teacher with all kinds of stuff and assists the students too. Sometimes, she gives our art board cool topics, and we draw or paint pictures on the topic. She decorates the board with the artwork. Two weeks ago, our topic was "My Neighborhood," and my class drew pictures of our neighborhoods. We haven't had a new topic yet, so our neighborhoods are still on the board for another week. We had fall photos taken last month, and Mrs. Lemon helped fix the hair or clothing of some kids before they got their picture taken.

About a year ago, I learned that volunteers don't get paid. When you volunteer, you do it because you like what you are doing and you have time to do it. You don't want anything in return. Volunteers just want to help other people.

My mom worked last summer at the Beverly State Home, a place where elderly people live. I thought she had a job and was going to get paid, but I found out that she just wanted to be of service to some people who needed her help. She was volunteering.

Last Saturday night, my family and I saw a play at the church of Mr. Wright (or Brother Wright, as my dad calls him). Brother Wright is my dad's good friend. The youth ministry was doing a play called "I See You, Jonah." Mr. Wright told my dad not to be late so that my sister and I would have good seats.

My dad did just that. He got to the church thirty minutes early. I was not sure we were early when I saw all the cars in the parking lot, but I soon found out that the cars belonged to the people in the play and all who were there as volunteers.

As we walked toward the church front door, I said to myself, "That looks like Mrs. Lemon." And I was right. It was her.

"Hello, Olivia, how are you?"

"I'm good."

"Well, it's good to see you outside of school."

"It's good to see you too."

Mrs. Lemon gave my mom a program, walked us to the front, and pointed out where we were going to sit. "Will this be okay, Mr. and Mrs. Crawford?"

"This is just fine. Thank you." My mom and Mrs. Lemon hugged each other.

"She is a great help to our community," my mom said.

"She is," I said.

"Mrs. Lemon helps this community by working at the school and the after-school program. She also does volunteer work at the Beverly State Home. She encourages me to volunteer there. She has been ushering at this church for such a long time. Olivia, she does all of it as a volunteer and never gets a paycheck, yet the payment she gets is so much more." My mom smiled.

"So, Mom, what other way is she getting paid if not with money?"

As my mom looked in my eyes, I knew the answer would be more than just an answer. It would be a lesson. "Mrs. Lemon helps others from her heart and never looks for anything in return. That's a pretty special person, and when you give to others more than to yourself, God will reward you with joy."

"Joy?"

"Yes, Olivia, joy is a payment that can't be taken away from you. If I lose my job at the hospital, I would lose a paycheck, but if you do a job or service for someone without looking for a monetary or some kind of payment in return, your heart will be full of a feeling we call joy."

I asked my mom, "How old do you have to be to volunteer?"

"You're old enough." Mom smiled.

The play was very good that night. I was so glad to see it. I was also glad to see Mrs. Lemon. The joy she has is a great thing to have. After being in my class, it's hard to believe anyone would come back to help, yet on Tuesday and Thursday, Mrs. Lemon is always on time. Mom is right. It takes special people. I also know that it takes a special job as well.

"Receive a payment of joy. Being a volunteer for the school is one job that I'll never forget, and I told all the kids I have helped that they also helped me. The kids always ask me how. And I would say, 'When you help someone, you are helping yourself. Kindness is something that always comes back to the person that shows it,'" says Mrs. Lemon.

Mr. Sino's Lasting Recipe

Saturday is my family night out for dinner. It's the day my dad provides dinner, so we eat out most of the time. I really like going to Mr. Sino's place to eat. Mr. Sino makes the best egg rolls, and he always gives us more than we order. Then he says to me, "You need more meat on your bones."

Mary, Mr. Sino's youngest daughter, is my age. We play at school together just about every day. When my church had a Sunday school rally, the Sinos came with their church members to help. Mr. Sino was in charge of the refreshments, but he wasn't by himself. Mary has two sisters and two brothers, and Mrs. Sino keeps everything in order.

That Saturday was the only Saturday I can remember that I saw Mr. Sino's food outside his restaurant, but just like the restaurant, the food was really good. The rally was from eight in the morning until two in the afternoon, and the Sinos worked very hard to feed over a hundred people. Mr. Sino, also a Sunday school teacher at his church, was glad to be a part of this rally.

Mrs. Sino took over the cooking when Mr. Sino had to teach the youth group. Mr. Sino started the class by asking if everyone enjoyed what they had for breakfast and lunch.

"Yes!" yelled the group of kids all together.

"Glad to hear it. In my hand, I have a recipe book that has the ingredients for your life. This book was passed on from family members to family members, friends to friends, strangers to strangers, and even people whom we may not call as friend for many, many years." Mr. Sino put out his arm with the Bible in it.

A girl named Angela asked, "Why would anyone call the Bible a recipe book? My mother said it's holy."

"Your mother is indeed right. This is a holy book, and no other book on earth will you hear the voice of God in like the Bible. It has all we need to help us live our lives here on earth the way God would have us to. I'm a chef, and when I get a recipe, old or new, it has to have the best ingredients, not just the right ones, for it to taste the best it can. And that's the difference between the Bible and other books. It teaches us the best way to live.

"All kinds of recipe fill the Bible. The book of Proverbs is just one of the books in the Bible that will give you the recipe to God's wisdom. And like Proverbs, other books in the Bible can help you in your everyday relationship with others and God. Now my friends, as you read your Bible from now on, just try to see how many recipes you can find for your life that will make it better for you and those all around you."

As Mr. Sino ended his class, the last thing he said was—and I believe it was the icing on the cake—"Friends, as a chef, recipes are a part of my everyday life. And as a Christian, I know the Bible is the sweetest recipe I ever came across. And one recipe I never had to change was God. He made it perfect the first time, and I never have to take out or add to His recipe. Now go and have a sweet life, my friends, because life can be sweet if you have the right ingredients from the right recipe."

Mr. Sino ended his class, handing each of us his favorite sweet to eat, fudge brownies.

By the way, he makes the best brownies I ever had. I have to get that recipe for my mom.

A Day of Cleanup

Amiya is the one person in my class who always seems to do everything just right. That's how it looks to me. My good friend and neighbor Pablo is the one person I know who can play all sports better than any other boy I know our age. Pablo is big in size, but his heart is the biggest part of him.

Mr. Fitch is the best workshop teacher a boy or girl could have. I have never seen anyone that works with wood who could build anything pretty much with his eyes closed. I have seen a few people in person and on TV, but Mr. Fitch is still the best carpenter in my eyes.

The third Saturday of each month, Amiya, Mr. Fitch, Pablo, and me (Sidney), along with some other church members, go to our community park to do a day of cleaning. We get there about seven, just before most of the people start to come out. Almost every time I go, I see someone from my school or neighborhood.

They mostly say the same thing to me, "Whose mess are you cleaning up?"

Almost every time, I say, "I'm cleaning up after whoever didn't clean up after themselves." But today, I want to know what my friends say when they are asked, "Whose mess are you cleaning?"

So while hard at work, picking up soda cans and any other trash left behind, I ask Amiya, "Hey, Amiya, what do you say when people ask you, 'Whose mess are you cleaning up?'"

Amiya stops what she is doing and looks me right in my eyes. "I tell them I'm cleaning the mess of people who have no respect for themselves or their community, and then I give them a big smile," Amiya says with no hesitation.

I think, *Just like Amiya to tell it like it is.*

I continue working until I get closer to where Pablo is working.

"Hey, man," I say, my way of greeting one of the guys.

"Hey, what's up?" Pablo replies.

"While working out here, does anyone ask you why you clean the park?"

"Yes, all the time. About three people already today."

"How do you respond?"

"I just simply say I enjoy coming to the park with my family and friends. And if I have to help keep it clean because some people are too lazy to pick up after themselves, then I say that maybe they would like to help one day."

"That's good, Pablo."

We fist-bump, and I think, *What a smart and very cool guy. So smart to let them know they also could help.*

It looks to me that Amiya and Pablo have the exact feeling about this community park cleaning day as I do. Thirty minutes pass before I see Mr. Fitch, and he is putting trash bags in the truck.

"Hi, Sidney. How are things going?"

"Going fine, Mr. Fitch."

"Glad to hear it."

He always speaks loud. My dad says it's because he can't hear very well, so he doesn't know how loud he is talking.

"Mr. Fitch, may I ask you a question?"

"Yes, sir."

"Do people ask you why you clean the park?"

"Sure they do. Someone just did before you came. Some people just don't understand why anyone would do anything if he weren't getting paid or getting something back in return for his time and work. From your expression, it looks like you already ran into some of those people."

"Well, I guess you could say that. When I'm cleaning the park, somebody from my school or neighborhood asks me why I'm doing it. So I tell them, 'Yes, sir. I do.'"

"Well, son, as long as you tell them and you know what you are saying is right. Maybe a few will remember and they will find something they can do to help our community. That's how I got involved with this weekend park cleaning." Mr. Fitch continues to talk without stopping to put the bags in the truck. "Your father was talking to a young man at church about doing for others. I realize I also had to stop thinking of just my family and me. I need to make this community a place we all can be proud of. We must be helpers to one another."

The answer from my three good friends does not surprise me. My pops told me a few years ago that the people you consider friends tells others a great deal about you. I believe my friends are caring, kind, and so much fun to be around. I believe my pops is right. I'm a lot like my friends. I've also been told I'm just like my pops. The next time anyone asks me why I'm cleaning up the park, I'll simply say, "I'm doing it for us all."

Debora's Gift

For many kids, Christmas is the day when they get their favorite gift of the year, but not for Debora. Her favorite gift of the year came months before Christmas. She would say, "This is the one gift that made God a lot closer to me, and I'm glad I didn't have to wait until Christmas to get it."

Her parents notice that six-year-old Debora is not seeing as well as she should. The eye doctor agrees with her parents when they took her to get her eye exam. The doctor tells Debora's parents that she is having a hard time seeing far away and glasses would help her. Debora's parents then tell her that she would be getting glasses soon to help her see better.

"Glasses," Debora repeats.

"Yes," her parents say at the same time in the same tone.

"But why?" Debora asks in a tone much like her parents before.

"Your eyes are not as strong as they need to be to see far way," Dad says, "and your eyes are doing too much work to see.

"Glasses will help your vision," her mom says.

Two days later after lunch, Debora and her parents are going to pick up her new glasses. Debora's father was already at work for about three hours when he called to say he would meet them at the eye doctor at one fifteen.

"Mom, will my glasses help me see people better?"

"Yes, Debora, they will help you see everything much better."

"Mom, will I see God better with my new glasses?" Debora asks with that tone of voice that is just like her parents when they talk about something important with her.

Her mom stops taking the things out of a black purse and putting them into a brown purse to answer, "Well, my little apple."

Her mother calls her "apple" because, when Debora was born, her face was as red as an apple. And Debora's grandfather says she is as red and sweet as a pretty red apple.

"I believe God is all around us, Apple. Everything you see that is good is a view of God."

Debora's mom continues to put her things in the brown purse, and Debora looks on as if she isn't concerned about the transfer taking place to one purse to the other. But it's as if she has something else on her mind.

"Mom, do you think my glasses will also help me see my mistakes better?"

Her mom looks up from what she is doing again. "Debora, your glasses are for your eyes, not your daily action. And what mistakes are you talking about, honey?"

"Mistakes like not flushing the toilet when I'm done."

"No, Apple. You just need to try to remember that. And I don't believe that is a mistake, honey. It's something you just need to work on doing, okay? Now let's go meet your dad."

As soon as Debora's mom pulls up to the eye center parking lot, she sees her husband's car. "Your dad is here."

"Yes, Mommy. I see him, and I don't have my glasses yet." Debora smiles.

"Hello, my two favorite girls in the world." Debora's father has a big smile on his face.

"Hi, honey," Debora's mother replies.

"Daddy, you beat us here." She gives him a huge hug, as if to say, "You're my favorite person too."

"So, Apple, are you ready to pick up your good-looking glasses?"

"Yes, Daddy, but my glasses are pretty, not good looking."

"Pretty, that's right. Just like you."

They all smile as they enter the eye center.

Debora talks all the way home, mostly about how she picked out the prettiest glasses in the center. "They really work. I can see much better with them. I didn't know my eyes were so sick until I put them on."

That night at bedtime, Debora's parents walk to her room to pray and say good night. As they enter, they see that Debora is looking out her window, smiling.

"Apple, what are you looking at?" her dad asks softly.

"I'm looking at heaven, and I already thank God for my new glasses. They really work. God showed me his favorite two cooking pots."

Debora's parents look out the window along with her.

"Do you see them, Daddy?"

"Yes, honey, I see them."

"Mom, do you think God made my eyes weak just so He could give me these glasses and I could see things that would bring Him closer to me?"

"I know God wants to be close to you, and I know He is very happy that you're feeling closer to him."

"I think my glasses are an early Christmas gift from God."

"You may be right about that, honey. Time for bed now," Debora's mom says.

When Debora gets in her bed, her dad gives her mom a wink, and her mom returns a wink back. Debora takes off her glasses and puts them on the nightstand by her bed.

When they finish praying, Debora looks at her parents. "I know that parents are the best gift from God, but glasses have to be my second because they help me to see my first best gift better."

"You're the best gift, Apple," her mom replies with watery eyes.

"Good night, Mom. Good night, Dad."

"Good night," Debora's parents say with that tone in their voice when something is important.

Soldier to Soldier

My name is James, and my father is a soldier in the United States Army. He spends a lot of time at work because that is what his job requires at this time, which means he spends a lot of time away from home. It's not easy for my family. My mom, little sister, and I know my dad's job is nothing like a regular nine-to-five job.

Three years ago, my dad had to go away to war. It was a very scary time for me and many kids whose dads had to go. It didn't matter to me why we were at war. All I could think about was if my dad and the other kids' dads were going to be okay. Living in Germany was pretty cool until that day I was told my dad was going to war.

I tried to be strong for my mom and sister, but I really needed to be strong for myself first. The night before my dad had to go, tears fell down my face as if I just had broken a bone. The pain was all in my heart. My heart was breaking. Dad came in my room, and my family prayed together like we did every night.

I was more focused on what my parents were saying this night more than any other night before. Dad prayed that God would watch over each of us and He had all things in His mighty hands. Then after each of us prayed, my mother took my sister to her room.

Tears began to fall more than before, and my dad hugged me and said, "James, I love you and thank God for you." My dad began to cry.

I laid my head on his chest as he continued to talk. He told me how proud he was of me and how I was a very mature boy for the age of eight. Then he said a few things that would stick with me, and I replayed what he said in my mind over and over while he was gone (and still do today).

"James, I'm a soldier in this world and a servant for my country, but I'm also a soldier for God, a servant for the commander-in-chief of the universe. The wars of this world will end. Good and evil is at war every day, and I want you to know, soldier to soldier, that you have to get up each day knowing that evil would like to see us unhappy and in pain. So we must fight evil with good. We can do that by loving the unlovable, helping the helpless, and telling others about the goodness of Jesus, which is the most important of all. James, this will take a mind of a soldier to do each day. Son, as I go away, we both have to have the same positive thinking. Evil will not overtake good, not when you're in the army of the Lord." Then he looked straight in my eyes and said it again, just as firm as before. "Soldier to soldier."

After eight months away, my dad came home, and it was a week before Christmas. We had a wonderful time. As I looked at my sister's wooden soldier ornament and the smiles that were on each family member's face, I knew the war had not ended. My family would not let down their weapon of love, and evil would not overcome us because we were soldiers.

I'm four years older now, and my dad is away again. It hasn't been any easier being without him. Even though I'm older now and know just how to get through these tough times without him, he is my best friend as well as my brother.

You may wonder how he can be my dad, best friend, and brother. We have the same commander-in-chief on earth and in heaven, but the one in heaven is also the Father to us both. That makes us brothers. I can talk with my dad about anything, and that is what you do with your best friend. So that's how he became all three to me

I may not go in the military like my dad, but I think that, if I continue to listen to him, I'll always be a soldier, one that will fight evil with good, love the unlovable, and help the helpless. And like I'm doing now, I will tell others how a soldier of the commander-in-chief of the universe can make life better even in times of war.

So I end by saying, "Soldier to soldier, evil will never overtake good."

A Prayer from Anna

Rose, the oldest out of six kids in my family, has a little more to do when it comes to helping at home this last year since our dad died. Rose never complains, and I have never seen any sign that she could be complaining on the inside. Reese is the next to the oldest. Then we have Ron and me, Andrea. And after me is Anna, and the youngest is Anthony. "My three Rs and my three As" is what my mother calls us sometimes.

I heard the most heartfelt prayer from my sister Anna, who needs a little more care than other girls her age. Because she was born blind, she needs care that kids who see just don't need. But a little more help is all truly she needs. Anna really can do pretty much everything for herself without help from anyone.

When fall break came, we had a great deal to do at my house—fall cleaning and yard raking. And my mother wanted walls painted and all the bedrooms this fall.

So the weekend before break, a family meeting was called. My mother had a plan. She said, if we did as she planned, we would be done in the two weeks we had. Mother had a good plan, and she didn't forget to add the fun stuff too.

My brothers were all for raking the yard and all the outside cleaning, but they were not looking forward to the inside work. When Mother made it very clear that everyone would help in all areas, outside and inside, the look on the boys' faces was evident that they didn't like that part of Mother's plan. Reese, being the oldest brother, would have to be a good example for the two younger boys.

My mother made it clear. "Reese, your brothers will need your guides. I know you will lead them well." Mother always had a way to make you feel that you had the best in you, and she was sure to see it.

After the family meeting, we had an awesome dinner. Mother fixed her favorite baked chicken, potato salad, green beans she canned last summer, and her homemade rolls. Yum! Eating all together at my house is a must. It was my dad's favorite time of the day. "Let's eat" was his favorite thing to say of the day.

My dad died a year ago in a four-car accident. We miss him so much, and not a day goes by that we don't talk about him. Dinnertime is perhaps the time of the day we think about him the most.

We had a great weekend. We went to the movies, bowled, and just spent time together. Mother reminded each of us that Monday would be the beginning of our home fall cleanup week.

"Let the games begin!" was how my mother greeted everyone that Monday morning.

After breakfast, we all had to look on the information board on the kitchen wall to see what our jobs for the day would be. The note from Mother began with, "Good morning, my three Rs and three As. It's a wonderful day to be outside, so we will begin our cleaning outside." Mother had a list of things to do with our names beside each duty we had to do. She ended the note the same way she greeted us. "Let the games begin!"

First on the list was raking the yard and bagging leaves. The boys had raking by their names, and the girls had bagging by ours. Mother was right. It was a very nice day to be outside. The sun was shining like a summer day, but the temperature was fifty-seven. It would reach a high of sixty-eight, so it was indeed a great time to do outside work, just like Mother said.

Praying is a part of my family life. My parents taught us all from a young age how to pray, so before we begin our jobs, saying a prayer was a natural thing to do.

Mother asked, "Who would like to lead us in prayer today?"

Anthony's hand was the first one up.

"Okay, Anthony, my little prayer warrior." Mother called him that because his hand was always the first one up.

Anthony began praying the same way he always did now that my dad was no longer with us. "God, tell Dad we miss him. Lord, bless my family with all the blessings You promise in my Bible. Keep us in Your care, and if we get hurt or even die like our dad did, help us to remember that You still love us. And Lord, let this fall break be a good one, and let us help our mother as much as we can so she won't be too tired. Thank You, God, for my mother, Rose, Andrea, Anna, Ron, and Reese. Amen."

I heard my Auntie Rose, who my sister was named after, once tell my three younger siblings that God still loved them. And because they were sad about our dad, they were to know that God didn't do anything wrong to him and he was now in heaven with God. I didn't know what was said before she made that statement, but it sounded as if one or all of my young siblings were not happy with God. Anthony really remembered what she said because his prayers sounded as if he still trusted God for our family needs. He is pretty smart to be so young.

"Thank you, Anthony, for that prayer. I believe we are ready to get to work now," Mother said with a soft smile on her face, a sign to us all that she was thinking about my dad at that moment while she was talking to us.

As we walked out the door, one by one to the yard, the boys got the rakes and started to work right away as if we were in a race.

"Slow down, guys! You're acting like this is a contest." Rose was trying not to laugh at them.

It was funny to see my brothers rake the yard as if someone had pushed the forward button on the DVD. I could not stop myself, and I wasn't alone. Rose laughed shortly after me.

The day outside was smooth sailing. Everything was just as Mother had said it would be if we followed her directions.

"Just one more day outside, and we'll be ready to start inside," Mother said that night before we all went to bed.

"Rise and shine and give God the glory, glory," Mother sang a couple of times.

It was a little harder getting up the next morning. The day before really did go smoothly, but we felt the work on our bodies today. Anna was the first up after Mother. Anna told Mother one day that she didn't want us to be waiting on her because it took her longer to get herself ready.

Rose was the next up, and as she entered the bathroom, she reached to turn the light on, but the light bulb was blown out. She got out a new bulb to put it in while she twisted out the old bulb. Ron, not seeing what she was doing, flipped the light switch. Sparks came out, and from what Ron said, he saw Rose fall to the floor.

Mother and all of us heard the fall. Everyone ran toward the bathroom, and Rose was on the floor, not moving. Reese called 9-1-1 without anyone telling him to, and Mother asked us to go downstairs and wait for help.

Anthony was saying over and over, "Rose isn't moving. Rose isn't moving."

As I heard Anthony repeat "Rose isn't moving," I looked at Ron, Reese, and then Anna. I saw Anna walk to the living room and sit down. She began to pray. I heard, "Father God, as you know, my family talks to You often, and it's not just when things are bad. But right now, I think You are the only one here who knows how bad things may or may not be. Rose is the nail in all our lives. She keeps us all looking toward better days after our father's death.

"She only says things that would keep us trusting in You and seeking You for all our needs, God oh God. My mother needs her more than anyone else. I'm asking You. Please let Rose be healed right now from any injury. Let her get up off the bathroom floor and walk down the stairs. God, I know Your will must come before mine, and You know better than I what is best for our family. I know families lose family members every day and sometimes more than one member at the same time, but I come asking You to have mercy on my family this day.

"Rose is the oldest, and she and Mother are very close. And now that Dad is with you, Mother needs a best friend. Rose has been that best friend. Mother can trust and depend on her, just like she did with Dad. God, talk with my dad, and I'm sure he would agree with me. Thank You. We won't be mad at You if You don't answer this prayer because we know in our hearts that You love our family. Amen."

I was not sure if I should let Anna know that I was listening to her, so I kept quiet. I mostly wanted her to keep praying. And if she knew I was listening, she might have stopped. Anna's prayer was answered as soon as she said "Amen."

I heard people walking down the stairs. Rose was on her feet, walking with the help of two medical people with Mother following behind, as close as she could possibly get.

Anthony began to clap his hands. "She's okay. She's okay. Look, guys. She's okay."

We all began to clap.

Two days passed, and Rose was home from the hospital and doing well. She was shocked and lucky to be here, as one doctor told Mother. Mother didn't tell us that information, but I heard her tell Aunt Rose on the phone. But mom said the doctor said "lucky."

She told Aunt Rose that the mercy of God, not luck, was why Rose was still here. God had mercy not just on Rose, but on all of us. I didn't hear her, but Aunt Rose surely said "Amen."

That night, we all met in Rose's bedroom for night prayer, and we all thanked God for Rose and allowing her to still be here with us. Anna prayed, but it was very short.

She just said, "God, thank You for hearing me."

And as we began to walk out of Rose's room, Anna and I headed to our room.

Anna said to me, "Andrea, thank you for not interrupting while I was talking with God when Rose was shocked."

I started to ask, "How did you know?" but Anna said, "You must forget that people who can't see actually hear really well. I could hear you breathing, and your heart was beating fast also."

I just said, "You're welcome, and I love you."

"I love you too," Anna said.

I held Anna's hands down the hall, which I never did, but I knew Anna wouldn't mind because I wasn't helping her down the hall. I was just letting her know that I was glad she let me know she didn't mind I heard her prayer.

Printed in the United States
By Bookmasters